For Justin Quigley. You are the one who inspired me to write this story. I love you sweetheart! <3

Once upon a time, there was a guy named Justin Quinton who was a superhero named Autisome. Justin works in the Autism department for a part-time job, since he's still in high school, to help people with autism become higher functioning. He also really helps families who can't afford therapy by helping to organize charities and fundraisers.

Justin is really supportive of the Autism department because some of his friends, including himself, have autism. His girlfriend Ariel Nelsen has it as well. Both Justin and Ariel only have mild autism, which means they are high functioning and can still do several things that people without disabilities can do. They have known each other since they were in elementary school but Justin was two grades ahead and two years older than Ariel.

Even though they go to different schools and mostly see each other on weekends, they still make each other feel happily special. Their families are also very supportive of them and Justin and Ariel feel blessed to have each other in their lives.

Before Justin became Autisome, he discovered that he could shoot a glow out of his hands. The glow had the colors of red, yellow, dark blue, and light blue. When he shot the glow on his bedroom wall he noticed that it showed a puzzle piece.

Justin shot the glow on his arm to see what it would do to him and he was really nervous that something bad would happen. But instead he felt really calm and relaxed. Then he started to believe that he had some special autistic power because the colors and the puzzle piece of the glow represented the autism spectrum.

One day, Justin walked past a school for kids with autism and he noticed that a little boy fell off a swing and started crying.

Justin shot the glow at the little boy so he could feel better and made sure no one saw him too.

Justin decided to keep his special power a secret because he didn't want people to think that he was dangerous by shooting the glow out of his hand. He didn't want to keep his autistic power a secret from his family, but he didn't know how to tell them.

When Justin was at his dad and stepmom's house, his little brother Will was crying because he had a lot of homework that he didn't want to do. His dad Michael and stepmom Lauri tried to calm Will down but Justin told them to let him calm down Will.

Then Justin shot his special glow at Will and he stopped crying and felt more calm. Lauri and his dad were in shock and asked Justin how he calmed Will down like that. Then Justin explained how it happened but he still didn't know how he got his autistic power.

Justin was surprised that his autistic power actually worked because Will didn't have autism. It made him wonder why the glow represented the autism spectrum. He started to wonder if it was just because he had autism, but still had no idea how he got his power in the first place.

Then he realized that he hadn't told his mom Tori about his special power yet since his parents were divorced.

When Justin was at his mom's house, Tori was in a really bad mood because she lost her iPhone. Then Justin shot his special glow at her and she felt calmer but was also really shocked.

Justin then explained to her how he discovered his special power and what he has been doing with it. Tori was really surprised that Justin had a special autistic power and she was really happy that his power wasn't dangerous and that it could help people by relieving them from pain, stress, and anxiety.

Later on she forgot about her phone and got all excited when Justin found her phone on Kiki's scratching pole. Kiki is Justin and Tori's lazy and always grumpy looking cat.

When Justin came to work at the Autism department, he decided to share his special power with the people he works with. Justin told everyone what he'd been doing with his power and he shot the glow out of his hands and it hit the roof. Everyone was shocked but they believed that his power was real.

Justin's boss asked him if he could publish his power in an article, and also help people with autism feel better when they're having a hard time during therapy sessions. Justin agreed to do it, but he said that he'd only be available during his normal working hours. Then his boss made an agreement with him.

A week before Justin's secret power was about to be revealed to everyone he went to visit Ariel's mom's house because Ariel was feeling depressed. When Justin arrived at Ariel's house, he asked her how she was doing and Ariel told him that she was feeling stressed with school.

Justin told her that he could make her pain go away and he shot his special glow at her. Then Ariel was feeling better and she asked him how he did it. Justin told her the story and she felt very happy that he was going to be like a superhero helping people.

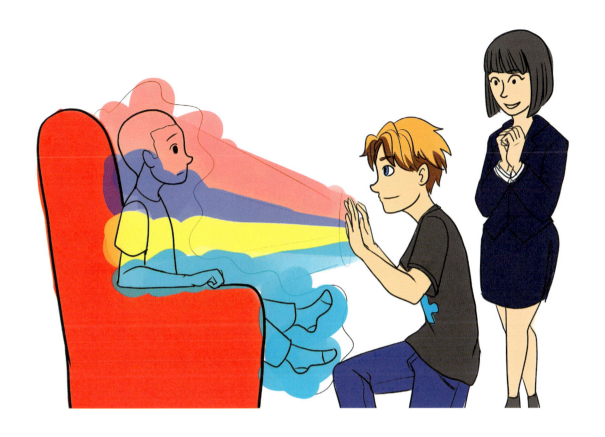

When Justin's special power was finally revealed, people started to tell him how fortunate it was for everyone to have his help. And he loved helping people who were going through a hard time during their therapy sessions at the autism department.

However, Justin started to have social problems with some people. Now that the public knew about his power and autism, people were bullying Justin by saying that he's a mentally disabled freak. Justin started to feel insecure with himself and he felt like quitting his job and being Autisome.

His family told him not to give up and reminded him that having autism makes him special and not less than any other person. Justin realized that his new power didn't change that and he also remembered that there were lots of other people in his life who were supporting him. So he continued helping people at the autism department, including his family and friends.

Even though some people try to bring Justin down for his special power and mental disability, he still remembers who he really is. So he keeps doing what he loves, he's thankful for all the people who support him, and he's proud of who he is. The autism department also published an article saying, "Your Autistic kids will be more awesome, thanks to Autisome." And that's how Justin got his superhero name.

Printed in Great Britain
by Amazon.co.uk, Ltd.,
Marston Gate.